Biking
An Outdoor Adventure Handbook

Biking

An Outdoor Adventure Handbook

Hugh McManners

DK

A DK PUBLISHING BOOK

Editor Patricia Grogan **Art Editor** Lesley Betts
Project Editor Fiona Robertson
Photography Susanna Price
US Editor Camela Decaire
Production Charlotte Traill

Managing Editor Jane Yorke
Managing Art Editor Chris Scollen

Cycling consultant Tony Yorke

The biking adventurers:
Laurence Gould, Roxanna Kashfi,
Mark Smith, Amelie Sumpter

First American Edition, 1996
2 4 6 8 10 9 7 5 3 1

Published in the United States by
DK Publishing, Inc., 95 Madison Avenue, New York, New York 10016
Visit us on the World Wide Web at http://www.dk.com

A CIP catalog record is available from the Library of Congress.

ISBN 0-7894-1105-9

Color reproduction by Colourscan, Singapore
Printed in Hong Kong by Wing King Tong

Contents

6
How to use this book

8
Which bike?

10
Fully outfitted

12
Equipping your bike

14
Getting ready to ride

16
Starting out

18
Ups and downs

20
Coping with obstacles

22
On your obstacle course

24
Fun and games

26
How to read a map

28
Planning your route

30
Navigating on your bike

32
Preparing for your trip

34
Recording your trip

36
Bike cleaning and oiling

38
Repairing a puncture

40
Maintaining your bike

42
First aid

44
Rules for the road

46
Glossary & Useful
addresses

48
Index & Acknowledgments

How to use this book

This book contains all the information you need to be safe and to have fun cycling. You'll see all the skills and techniques you should practice for on- and off-road riding, and find lots of useful hints, tips, and ideas.

Getting started

Before setting off on a cycling trip, you will need to get the right bike. But going into a bike shop can be very confusing – there are lots of bikes to choose from, and many different bike accessories. This section gives you the basic information you need.

Learn what the differences are between a mountain bike and a racing bike on page 9.

Make the tool pouch on page 13 to store your tool kit in.

Look on page 15 to learn how to feather your brakes.

Make the limbo bar on page 21 to practice cycling under low obstacles.

Back to basics

Biking off-road can be even more challenging than biking on-road. You never know when you will have to cycle over an obstacle or up a steep hill. Learning how to use your brakes and gears properly will help you cope in any situation.

Ready for anything

Practice makes perfect. Build an obstacle course at home to practice your cycling skills. This will give you the confidence to tackle rough ground when you are out on a trail. You can also hone your skills by playing games on your bike with your friends.

Test your cycling skills on the obstacle course shown on page 22.

Make the baton on page 25 to use when playing cycle polo.

Make the map case on page 28 to store your map in.

Learn how to make a route card and discover its use on page 29.

Exploring new areas

Being able to find your way with a map and a compass will enable you to explore new areas on your bike. This section teaches you how to plan a route, determine how long it will take you to cover it, and be sure you set off in the right direction.

Planning a trip

Going on a cycling trip is probably one of the most exciting adventures you can have on your bike. You'll need to be prepared for any changes in the weather and must have plenty to drink. You could make a logbook to record your adventure.

See page 32 to learn how to make a cycle cover to protect your bike.

Look on page 34 for instructions on making a logbook.

Safe biking

Learn how to repair a puncture on page 38.

Find out how to get grit out of your eye on page 42.

You need to take care of your bike with regular cleaning, oiling, and basic maintenance. A poorly maintained bike can be dangerous. It is also important to know how to perform first aid in case of an accident.

Finding out more

Lots of people enjoy cycling and there are lots of organizations that can help you get started. When you do get out on the road or trail, be sure you know the basic rules – respect the countryside and clean up after yourself so others can enjoy it too.

Use the glossary on page 46 to look up useful biking terms.

The index on page 48 shows you where to find everything in this book.

How to use each page

Each double-page in this book explains everything you need to know about one subject. The introduction gives you an overview, and the step-by-step instructions show you how to make, do, and practice all the activities.

 Star symbol
This symbol draws your attention to important safety points.

Wheel symbol
You will see a wheel symbol next to every useful hint, tip, or additional piece of information.

The colored band on each page reminds you which section you are in. This page is in the Planning a trip section.

Step-by-step instructions show you how to make and do everything in stages.

Locater picture
This picture sums up what is being covered on the double-page.

Materials box
Most pages have a materials box. Look here to see what materials you will need for each project or activity.

Page name
The name of the double-page is printed in the top right-hand corner. This will help you find the correct page when flipping through the book.

Hints and tips
Each hints and tips box is full of useful information.

Hints and tips boxes have a picture of a boy or a girl. Most pages have one of these boxes.

Boxed pictures
The instructions underneath these pictures fill in the details on how to make and do the activities.

Extra information
The bottom right-hand pages often have additional or new information about the subject.

Which bike?

When you first start cycling, you do not need a very specialized bike, but you do need to be sure you get a bike that is appropriate for the kind of riding you plan to do. There are lots of different bikes to choose from and the various components can vary in quality, but all have some basic features in common.

When buying a bike, choose a store with a good selection.

The main features of a bike

Study the bike shown below to learn the names of all the different parts. This will help you understand how your bike works and what to ask for if you need to buy spare parts. This bike is a hybrid bike. It is a cross between a mountain bike and touring bike.

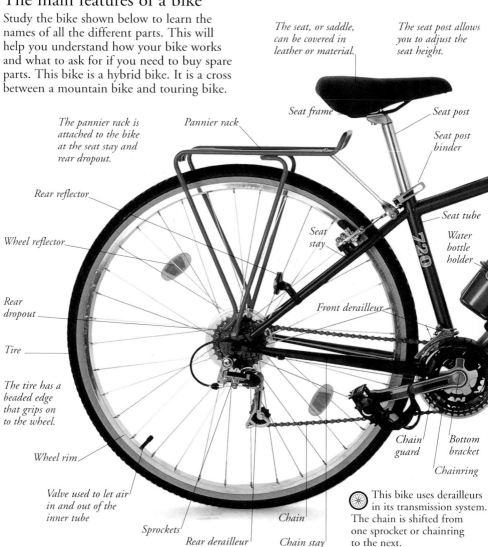

The seat, or saddle, can be covered in leather or material.

The seat post allows you to adjust the seat height.

The pannier rack is attached to the bike at the seat stay and rear dropout.

Pannier rack

Seat frame

Seat post

Seat post binder

Rear reflector

Wheel reflector

Seat stay

Seat tube

Water bottle holder

Rear dropout

Front derailleur

Tire

The tire has a beaded edge that grips on to the wheel.

Wheel rim

Chain guard

Bottom bracket

Chainring

Valve used to let air in and out of the inner tube

Sprockets

Rear derailleur

Chain

Chain stay

This bike uses derailleurs in its transmission system. The chain is shifted from one sprocket or chainring to the next.

Where to store your bike

If finding room to store your bike at home is a problem, you could buy an indoor bike rack. Some are freestanding, others attach to a wall. Ask an adult to help you set yours up. You can then hang your bike up to keep it out of the way.

The differences between three common bikes

A mountain bike has a sturdy frame and fat tires with a good grip for riding on rough ground.

○ Most modern bikes have quick-release levers, which allow you to adjust parts of your bike very easily.

○ Bearings contain small metal balls that enable parts of your bike to move smoothly.

○ There are several kinds of gear shifters, including thumb, under-bar, and grip shifters.

A racing bike is built for speed, so it has a very light frame and large, narrow wheels.

A cruiser is designed for riding on-road. A basket is often attached to the front.

Gear lever

Brake lever

The headset holds the front forks in the headtube.

Handlebar grip

The handlebars are usually flat.

Handlebar stem

Headset

Top tube

Brake cable

Head tube

Front reflector

Brake pad

Brake arm

Down tube

Water bottle

Cycle pump

Pedal

Front fork

Crank

Toe clip

The spokes support the wheel rim.

The quick-release lever attaches the wheel to the bike.

The hubs on the front and rear wheels contain bearings and hold the spokes.

Wheel reflector

○ The pedals have an uneven surface for extra grip.

○ Bikes with several gears usually have one, two, or three chainrings.

Spoke

All valves have a cap for protection.

○ If your wheels do not have quick-release levers, you will need to use a wrench to remove them.

Whether you are riding on- or off-road, always wear a cycling helmet.

Fully outfitted

Being safe and comfortable on your bike can make all the difference between an enjoyable ride and a miserable one. Your most important accessory is a well-fitting helmet to protect your head, but that is the only special equipment you need. Follow the guidelines below when choosing the rest of your gear.

Your second skin

Choose clothing that is close-fitting. Baggy clothes can get caught up in the moving parts of your bike. Be sure your gear is not so tight you cannot move however! Also, avoid pants with bulky seams in the seat area.

Choose a helmet that has been safety tested and is labeled accordingly.

A bandanna will help keep you cool in the summer and warm in the winter.

Wear several thin layers of clothes so that you can remove or add layers if you get too hot or cold.

Wear a light-weight sweater on cool days.

A cotton T-shirt will keep you cool in the summer.

Avoid V-neck sweaters as they do not keep your chest warm.

Always wear or pack a wind- and waterproof jacket.

Wear an undershirt under your top to absorb sweat when you are cycling.

Sweatpants or leggings will keep you warm on cool days.

If you plan to be out cycling for a long time, you will be more comfortable in cycling shorts than normal shorts.

Shorts are ideal for warm days.

Make sure your jacket is not too loose, otherwise it will flap around when you cycle.

Ideally, your jacket should have air vents to allow sweat to evaporate.

Cotton or wool socks will stop your feet from getting cold.

Wear shoes with a stiff sole so that the balls of your feet do not get sore when pedaling your bike.

How to make sure your helmet fits you correctly

Put the helmet on and fasten the straps. Check that it fits snugly and does not slide around.

If the chin strap is loose, your helmet will not stay in place when you cycle over rough ground.

When adjusting your straps, ensure both sides are adjusted equally.

The helmet should sit low over your forehead to protect it, but should not obscure your vision.

Special gear

Of all the special biking gear available, cycling shorts and shoes are the most useful items for general cycling.

Choose a cycling helmet that has comfortable straps.

A water bottle that fits onto your bike is the best way to carry drinks.

Wear a top that will keep your lower back covered when you lean forward on your bike.

Cycling shorts have a padded seat for extra comfort.

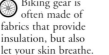

Cycling shorts fit very snugly and do not have any uncomfortable seams.

Cycling shoes have an extra-stiff sole.

Biking gear is often made of fabrics that provide insulation, but also let your skin breathe.

Cycling shoes designed for racing have a clip on the sole that fastens to the pedal.

How a bandanna can help keep you warm or cool

To absorb sweat, fold a bandanna in a triangle and wrap it around your neck.

The triangular part of the bandanna should cover the back of your neck to protect it from sunburn.

In cold weather, keep your head warm by wearing the bandanna under your helmet.

With the bandanna still folded, place it over your head and tie it at the nape of your neck.

Protecting your head and hands

Your head, eyes, and hands are most at risk from injury when cycling. A helmet is essential, and glasses and gloves are very useful.

Most helmets are made of polystyrene.

This helmet has good ventilation.

Open-fingered gloves give you the most control.

The adjustable padding makes the helmet more comfortable.

Eye protection
Sunglasses will protect your eyes from insects, mud, dust, and sunlight.

Cycling helmet
Look for a light-weight helmet that has good ventilation.

Cycling gloves
Wear cycling gloves to protect your hands from blisters.

Make sure your bike is properly equipped every time you go out.

Equipping your bike

Once you've outfitted yourself, you must also outfit your bike. A basic tool kit is essential – you never know when you may need to perform a simple repair. If you plan to ride at dawn or dusk, you will also need to equip your bike with lights and reflectors so that you can be seen easily.

Materials for the tool pouch

Needle   *Thread*

Scissors

Toe-clip straps

Oblong of material

Your essential tool kit

The items shown here will enable you to carry out basic repairs on your bike. If your bike needs any major work, take it to a bike shop to be repaired.

Multi-purpose oil

Keep a can of oil at home so that you can oil your bike after every wash.

Cycle pump

Choose a good quality pump that you can clip onto your bike frame.

Screwdriver

Wrench

Make sure your screwdriver is the correct size for the screws on your bike.

This multiheaded wrench will ensure that you have the correct-sized wrench for most repairs.

See page 13 for the contents of a puncture repair kit.

Hints and tips

Bungee cords and toe-clip straps are very useful for securing items to your bike.

Install a white light at the front of your bike and a red light at the back.

Measure your tools so that you know what size to make each section of your tool pouch.

Use plastic tire levers since they are lightweight.

Tire lever

There are several kinds of inner tubes, so check at a bike shop to see which kind you need for your bike.

Tire levers will help you remove the tire from the wheel when you are repairing a puncture.

Inner tube

Always take a spare inner tube with you in case you get a puncture.

Spoke wrench

A spoke wrench is used to tighten and adjust the spokes on your bike.

Chain tool

Allen wrenches come in several sizes.

A set of Allen wrenches, like the one shown here, is ideal – you will be sure to have the correct-sized wrench for most jobs.

A chain tool is used to remove rivets.

It is difficult to repair a broken chain, so ask an adult to help you.

How to make a tool pouch to store your tools in

Hem the oblong of material, then fold it so that the back section is larger than the front.

Sew the sides of the material together to make a pouch. Now divide the pouch into sections.

Sew straight lines through the material to secure the sections and slide the tools inside.

Fold the top of the tool pouch over and then roll the pouch up. Secure it with a toe-clip strap.

Bike accessories

Bike shops stock all the accessories you need for your bike. Some of the more important ones are shown here.

Bike computer

Bell

Some cycle bells have a simple compass that can help you tell direction.

Water bottle and holder

Front light

Reflective arm bands

Rear light

Reflective pant clips

Reflective stickers

Reflective body strap

All new bikes are equipped with reflectors.

Bicycle lock and keys

Bungee cords

Toe-clip straps

Avoid over-stretching a bungee cord – it could snap back on you.

Pannier rack

Toe clips

See page 33 to learn how to assemble a pannier rack.

Panniers that fit over the back wheel

How to attach your tool pouch to the bottom of your seat

Thread the toe-clip strap around the underside of the seat frame to make a loop.

Slide the rolled tool pouch approximately halfway through the looped toe-clip strap.

Pull the toe-clip strap tight to secure the tool pouch to the underside of the seat frame.

When cycling over rough ground, use two toe-clip straps to make the tool pouch extra secure.

Puncture repair kit

The most common repair you are likely to undertake is patching a puncture. You can buy puncture repair kits from all bike shops. Make sure the one you carry contains the items shown here.

Container for puncture repair kit

Sandpaper

Wax crayon

Chalk

Cement

See page 38 to learn how to repair a puncture.

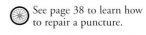

Large patches

Small circular patches

Getting ready to ride

Before you set off on a bike, be sure that it is the right size for your height and that every part of it is working properly. As long as the bike frame is the correct size, you can adjust the other parts of the bike to fit you comfortably. Ask an adult to help you. Then carry out the pre-ride checks listed below.

When sitting on your bike, the tips of your toes should just touch the ground.

Preparing your bike

If your bike is not adjusted to fit you, it will be very difficult to ride and could even be dangerous. It is equally important that all the parts of your bike be in working order.

What size?

You should be able to stand astride your bike with both feet on the ground. When sitting on the seat, you should be able to reach the handlebars easily while looking ahead.

See page 41 to learn how to adjust your handlebars.

Adjusting the angle of the handlebars may make it easier to reach the brake levers.

How to adjust the angle and height of your seat

Seat post binders are loosened using an Allen wrench or regular wrench, or a quick-release lever.

Loosen the seat post lever and adjust the seat to the correct height. Then tighten it again.

To adjust the seat angle, you'll also use an Allen wrench or regular wrench. Most seats are comfortable at a flat angle.

Hints and tips

Your tire sides should be very firm. If you can push them in, they need to be pumped up.

All seat posts have a safety line marked on them to indicate the maximum height to which you can move the saddle up.

You need to make sure the pedals on your bike have a good grip.

Pre-ride checks

Check your brakes, tires, lights, and reflectors before every ride. Once a month, give the other parts of your bike a thorough check.

Remember to adjust your seat height every few months because you are still growing.

Ask an adult to help you check your tires by squeezing in the sides.

See page 40 for details on checking the other parts of your bike.

The correct foot position with and without toe clips

Place the ball of your foot on the pedal and push your foot down to start pedaling.

Avoid placing the heel of your foot on a pedal as your foot could easily slip off.

Flick the pedal up with your foot to lift the toe clip and then slide your foot forward into the clip.

A toe clip will help keep your foot in the correct position and make it easier to cycle up steep hills.

When you first start using toe clips, use shallow ones without straps so that you can remove your feet easily.

With experience, you can learn to feather your brakes. Feathering is when you make rapid, gentle pulls on your brake levers.

Always look behind you to check for other riders or people before you start cycling.

Lean forward from the hips.

Ready to go

Now you are ready to learn basic cycling skills. Sit squarely on the bike seat, lean forward slightly, and keep your back straight.

Start off by pushing the ball of one foot firmly down on the pedal.

Practice starting off with each foot forward so you are comfortable starting from any position.

Keep your hands and arms relaxed.

1 For normal cycling, you should be able to hold your handlebars with your arms slightly bent and your hands shoulder-width apart.

Brake lever

Brake cable

Pull the brake levers toward you when you brake.

2 Check that you can pull on both brake levers comfortably. You may find it easier to keep your fingertips on the levers all the time.

Keep your weight back in your seat when you slow down.

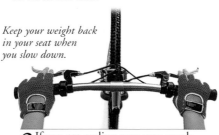

3 If you are cycling over very rough ground, keep two fingers on each hand on the brake levers so you are ready to brake quickly.

How the brake pads make your bike slow down

The cable that runs from each brake lever operates the two rubber blocks called brake pads.

Pull gently on the brake levers. The front edges of the brake pads should touch the wheel rim first.

When the brakes are fully on, the whole edge of each brake pad will touch the wheel rim.

An empty parking lot is a good place to practice your cycling skills.

Starting out

When you first start cycling, choose a quiet place to practice. Once you feel comfortable stopping, starting, and cycling in a straight line, try turning corners. This will develop your steering skills, and is also good practice for using your brakes. After this, you will be ready to learn how to use your gears.

Materials for the cones

Colored tape

Scissors

Poster board

Hints and tips

Use a low gear to cycle around the cones slowly and a medium gear to cycle around them quickly.

Try to turn each pedal around 80–90 times a minute. This is called your pedal cadence.

To figure out how many gears your bike has, multiply the number of chainrings by the number of sprockets.

When cycling slowly, slightly ease off the pressure on the pedals when you change gear.

Slalom cycling

Steering is one of the most important skills you need to learn. Practice steering in and out of cones at varying speeds – this will help you cycle around all kinds of obstacles off-road.

1 Make six cones, using the guide on the right. Place the cones about 6½ ft (2 m) apart in a zigzag shape. Now practice cycling in and out of the cones at varying speeds.

Approach each turn slowly to start with.

Lean into the turn from your hips.

Practice with your friends.

Use your brakes to control your speed.

If you feel you are losing your balance, put one foot down.

Turn the handlebars as smoothly as you can.

2 When you can do this confidently, move the cones closer together. You will have to steer more carefully to maneuver between the cones.

Try cycling around the cones quickly. You will find that the faster you cycle, the more you have to lean in to your turns.

How to make cones to practice cycling around corners

Roll one piece of oblong poster board diagonally to make a cone shape. Make sure it has a wide base.

Tape the cone together along the long edge. You may need a friend to hold the cone for you.

Trim the poster board around the bottom edge so that the cone stands fairly upright.

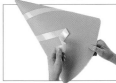

Decorate the cone with the colored tape. You could wrap it around the cone diagonally.

How to turn sharply to avoid unexpected obstacles

Place a cone on the ground and cycle toward it quickly, but still under control.

When you are about 6 ½ ft (2 m) from the cone, turn the handlebars very quickly toward it.

Immediately turn the handlebars in the direction you want to go around the obstacle.

By turning the handlebars in the opposite direction first, you can make a much sharper turn when cycling quickly.

Getting to know your gears

The gears on your bike will help you turn your pedals at the same speed whether you are cycling slowly along a narrow path or quickly down a steep hill.

When changing gears, keep pedaling, otherwise the chain may jam.

Practice feeling your gear changes rather than looking down at the gear shifter.

Gear shifter

Seven sprockets *Chain* *Large, middle, and small chainring*

The parts of your gear system

Most bikes have a derailleur gear system. If the bike has 21 gears, it will have three chainrings. seven sprockets, and one chain. The chain runs around one of the chainrings and one of the sprockets, depending on which gear you are in.

The front derailleur moves the chain across the chainrings.

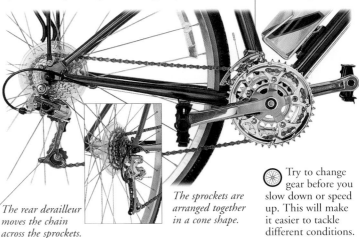

The rear derailleur moves the chain across the sprockets.

The sprockets are arranged together in a cone shape.

Try to change gear before you slow down or speed up. This will make it easier to tackle different conditions.

Two kinds of gear shifters on the handlebars

If your bike has a grip shifter, you will change gears by twisting the handlebar grip.

A thumb shifter is a small lever that you push or pull to change gears.

Low gears
When you use the small chainring and two or three of your largest sprockets, you are in a low gear. You will need a low gear when you are cycling slowly or climbing up steep hills.

Middle gears
You will use the middle gears most of the time. They will allow you to cycle quickly without too much effort. Use the middle chainring with any sprocket.

High gears
When you are cycling very quickly, use the high gears. You will need the large chainring and two or three of the smallest sprockets.

Ups and downs

Whether you are cycling along a narrow path or speeding down a steep hill, you must keep your bike under control at all times. Most accidents happen when cyclists race out of control. Avoid this by learning how to use your brakes and gears effectively.

Cycling across a slope requires very good balancing skills.

Materials for the chicane

Flowerpots

Garden stakes about 6 ½ ft (2 m) long

Hints and tips

As a general rule, the steeper the hill, the lower the gear you will need to cycle up it.

When doing an emergency stop off-road, pull on your back brake slightly harder than your front brake.

Pull on your front brake slightly harder than your back brake when performing an emergency stop on-road.

Making a chicane

A chicane is a tricky obstacle on a racecourse. Here you'll construct a simple chicane to help improve your balancing skills.

Put one end of the garden stake on the inside edge of the flowerpot.

Use a garden stake to measure the width of the chicane.

1 Place four flowerpots in an oblong shape that is about 1 ½ ft (50 cm) wide and 6 ½ ft (2 m) long. Balance one garden stake on top of two of the flowerpots.

Keep the two lines of garden stakes at an equal distance throughout the chicane.

2 Balance a second garden stake on the other two flowerpots. Add two more flowerpots about 6 ½ ft (2 m) farther along and balance two more garden stakes in the same way. Repeat this process until the chicane is about 20 ft (6 m) long.

3 Practice cycling through the chicane. Approach it slowly in a low gear. Push down firmly on the pedals and use the brakes to control your speed. Stay in an upright position – leaning to one side will knock you off-balance.

Sit squarely on the seat.

The narrower the chicane, the harder it is to cycle through.

Try cycling through the chicane standing on your pedals.

Cycling uphill

On gentle slopes you can sit or stand while cycling, but on steep hills you should try to remain seated all the way up. This helps the back wheel grip the ground firmly. When you stand up, it can spin out of control.

To cycle up a gentle slope, keep your weight far back in the seat and pedal with your heels down.

Grip the handlebars firmly.

On steep hills keep your weight in the center of the bike. Bend your arms and bring your head forward to stop the front wheel from lifting up.

Change into a lower gear before the hill gets steeper.

Cycling downhill

You can gain a lot of speed cycling down a hill, so it is important to stay in control. Always change into a middle gear, as shown on page 17, before you go down a hill, and use the brakes to control your speed.

Grip the handlebars firmly.

When cycling down a gentle slope, keep your arms straight and sit back in the seat.

Keep your knees bent and relaxed.

Pick out a smooth path before cycling down a hill.

Freewheel down steep hills by keeping your pedals level. Keep your speed under control by feathering the brakes.

If a hill is very steep, get off your bike and walk down.

Be sure you can use your brakes confidently before you set off on any ride.

Emergency stops

When you need to brake very quickly it is called an emergency stop. Slide back on your seat and pull gently but firmly on both brakes.

Practice braking in a straight line by cycling between two pieces of rope.

To start with, brake gently. Increase the pressure on your brakes as you slow down.

If you pull too hard on your back brake, you are likely to skid. This is because your back wheel will lock, putting you off-balance.

Pulling too hard on your front brake will make your bike tip forward. In extreme cases, you could even fly over the handlebars.

Coping with obstacles

Half the thrill of cycling off-road is coping with the changing conditions. You might find yourself cycling under low branches, carrying your bike over very rough ground, or even hopping over small logs. You need special skills to cope with these conditions, so learn the techniques shown here before you set off.

In some conditions, it may be more sensible to get off your bike and push it.

Materials for the cycle limbo

Colored tape

2 cones (see page 16)

Garden stakes 6 ½ ft (2m) long

Log

Hints and tips

Use toe clips to help you pull up the pedals when you are hopping over obstacles.

If you know you will have to carry your bike, try to keep it light by not attaching extra equipment to it.

When to carry your bike

If you come across ground that is so steep or bumpy you cannot cycle over it safely, you will need to get off your bike and carry it.

Always lift your bike from the left-hand side to avoid the greasy chainring and sharp sprockets on the right-hand side.

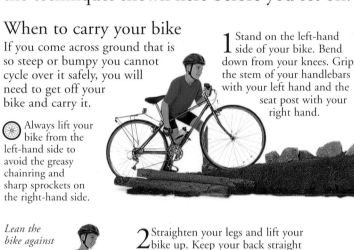

1 Stand on the left-hand side of your bike. Bend down from your knees. Grip the stem of your handlebars with your left hand and the seat post with your right hand.

Lean the bike against you.

2 Straighten your legs and lift your bike up. Keep your back straight and hold the bike firmly. Check that the wheels are far enough off the ground to clear any obstacles.

If you try to cycle over very rough ground, you could damage your tires.

3 If you are carrying your bike over very large boulders, you may need to lift it higher. Bend your right arm up, making sure you keep your elbow close to your side.

If you bump your bike when carrying it over an obstacle, check that nothing is damaged.

Check that the ground is firm before putting all your weight on it.

Hopping over logs

Tree roots and logs are some of the most common obstacles in the countryside. With practice, you can learn how to hop over these obstacles without getting off your bike.

Approach the log straight on.

1 Pedal slowly toward the obstacle. Move your weight over the back of the bike and, just before you reach the log, pull up on the handlebars to lift the front wheel off the ground. Push the pedals downward to give you more lift.

Use a low gear so that you have more control.

2 As soon as your front wheel has cleared the log, shift your weight forward again. This will bring your front wheel down and get you in position for lifting your back wheel over the log.

Make sure the obstacle is not wider than the distance between your wheels.

Keep your weight over the front wheel.

Press down on the handlebars.

3 Lift yourself out of the seat and pedal hard so that the back wheel lifts up off the ground. When you have cleared the obstacle, sit back in the normal riding position.

Pull gently on the front brake.

Push down hard on the lower pedal.

Practice cycling over a soft obstacle like a small cardboard box to start with.

How to make a limbo bar to practice cycling under low obstacles

Tape two small garden stakes about 12 in (30 cm) apart, at right angles to one large stake.

Repeat the first step and then balance another long garden stake along the two taped rods.

Cycle limbo

Cycling under a limbo bar is good practice for cycling under low branches when you are off-road.

Ultimate limbos
When the limbo bar is as low as 3 ½ ft (110 cm), you will have to come right off your seat. This takes a lot of bike control.

Lean your body to one side.

Look ahead.

Sit far back.

Put each upright garden stake in a cone (see page 16).

Approach the bar slowly and freewheel under it.

Use your arms to help you keep your balance when you lean to one side.

On your obstacle course

Competing on an obstacle course is an ideal way to test your cycling skills – it is a lot harder to tackle a series of obstacles than to get through one at a time! The obstacle course shown here will test a wide variety of the skills needed for on- and off-road cycling.

Cycling clubs regularly set up obstacle courses to test cycling skills.

Building your course

Pages 16–21 show you how to make all the sections of this course. Put the sections together as shown here.

Adapt the cones made on page 16 to make two starting posts.

Approach the cones with just enough speed to stop you from wobbling.

Tape a triangle of material or poster board to the top of the garden stake.

Take turns starting.

1 Position the cones made on page 16 in a curve. You will need to cycle in and out of the cones, so make sure you space them out enough – about 6 ½ ft (2 m) apart.

Make sure you do not cycle too close to the person in front of you.

As you gain more experience, move the cones closer together to make this section harder.

Ask a friend to time you with a stopwatch to see how long it takes you to complete the course.

2 Place the chicane made on page 18 after the cones. To start with, make the chicane approximately 3 ft (1 m) wide. As you gain more experience, make the chicane narrower.

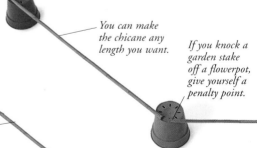

You can make the chicane any length you want.

If you knock a garden stake off a flowerpot, give yourself a penalty point.

You will need to cycle very slowly in order to maneuver your bike through the chicane.

You could use cardboard boxes instead of flowerpots.

Some of the skills you will need for cycling on a trail

Use the skills you learned cycling under the limbo bar to cycle under low branches off-road.

If the ground is rough and uneven, it is often easier to get off your bike and push or carry it.

Use the skills you learned on the slalom to cycle around pot holes, boulders, and stones.

Cycling through the chicane is good practice for cycling along a narrow path.

7 Finish your obstacle course in style by making two finishing posts the same way you made the starting posts.

Make this obstacle harder by lowering the bar.

6 Make the limbo bar shown on page 23 and put it at the end of your obstacle course. Make it high to start with. Lower the bar as you gain more confidence.

5 Lay down two logs approximately 6 ½ ft (2 m) apart. Carry your bike over the logs as shown on page 20. When you get more experienced, practice cycling over the logs as shown on page 21.

As you gain more experience, move the cones closer together so that you have to turn in between them more sharply.

The faster you cycle around each cone, the more you will have to lean into the turn.

4 Position two more cones after the chicane. Cycle around these cones one-handed. This is good practice for when you are cycling on roads and need to give hand signals.

3 When the chicane is only 1 ½ ft (50 cm) wide, you will not be able to push the pedals in a complete circle. Get the pedals level and then push each one forward and backward about one quarter of a turn. Repeat this process to move through the chicane.

Use your brakes to control your speed around the obstacles.

This section requires a lot of balancing skill.

As you maneuver around the first cone, be careful not to knock the chicane with your back wheel.

Weaving in and out of cones is one of the most popular cycling games.

Fun and games

When you are cycling in a group, you should always be aware and considerate of the other cyclists. The games shown on these pages are not just fun to play, they are a good way to practice cycling with other people around. Choose a safe, out-of-the-way place to play these games.

Materials for the games

Flower-pots

Tape

Soft ball

Rope　*Scissors*

Newspaper

Hints and tips

Keep your bike in a low gear to help you cycle slowly.

Make sure every team member gets a chance to play.

Always keep a safe distance from the other competitors.

Cycle relay

You need two teams of at least two people each to do a cycle relay.

Place flowerpots at either end of each rope to mark the start and finish.

1 Lay three lengths of rope in straight lines 3 ft (1 m) apart. One person on each team starts at one end of the rope lanes, holding a soft ball, and cycles to the other end.

2 A second person from each team waits at the other end of the rope lanes to collect the ball from the first team member.

Pass the ball to the second team member.

Be ready to start cycling as soon as you have the ball.

Make sure each team member takes a turn cycling with the ball.

3 The second team member then cycles back to the other end of the rope lanes with the ball. The first person to cross the finish wins for his or her team.

Slow race

As its name suggests, this race is all about how slowly you can cycle. The last person to cross the finish line is the winner.

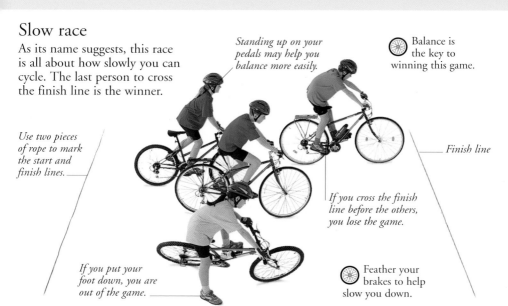

Standing up on your pedals may help you balance more easily.

Balance is the key to winning this game.

Use two pieces of rope to mark the start and finish lines.

Finish line

If you cross the finish line before the others, you lose the game.

If you put your foot down, you are out of the game.

Feather your brakes to help slow you down.

Cycle polo

Whether you are taking a drink from your water bottle or signaling a turn on the road, you will need to cycle one-handed at some point. Cycle polo is a fun game to play that will help your one-handed cycling skills.

Practice using alternate hands to bat with.

1 Position several flowerpots about 6 ½ ft (2 m) apart in a zigzag shape. Make a baton as shown on the left and get a soft ball.

Weave in and out of the flowerpots.

How to make a baton with newspaper for playing cycle polo

Ask a friend to time how long it takes you to complete the course.

Hit the ball very gently so that you have more control.

Take approximately five sheets of newspaper and roll them lengthwise to make a long tube.

2 The goal of the game is to bat the ball around the flowerpots. Take turns starting and leave at least 16 ft (5 m) between each cyclist.

You will need to practice turning your handlebars with just one hand.

Secure the tube by wrapping pieces of colored tape around it at 4-in (10-cm) intervals.

3 Always bat the ball ahead of you around the flowerpot and then cycle slowly after it. As you gain more experience, you can try cycling quickly around the obstacles.

Use your brakes to control your speed.

How to read a map

If you want to explore new areas on your bike, you should always take a map with you so you won't get lost. Maps show you the exact positions of objects and what the land, or terrain, is like. Study all the features on the map shown here so that you can learn how to read a map of your area.

Learn how to read a map so that you can explore new places.

Legend

Major road

Secondary road

Trail

Town

Bridge

Railroad line

Railroad station

Woodland

Lake

River

Marshland

Contour line

0–300 ft
300–650 ft
650–1,000 ft
Over 1,000 ft

Land-height bands

The north point shows you where north is on the map.

The legend tells you what all the symbols on a map represent.

Maps often use slightly different symbols to represent very different objects or features. Study the legend on your map carefully so that you know what each symbol represents.

Land height is shown in blocks of color on this map. This allows you to see changes in land height at a glance, and figure out where you'll find some big hills.

Several woodland symbols close together indicate a forest.

Study this map carefully and see if you can figure out an interesting route to cycle along. Try to avoid major roads.

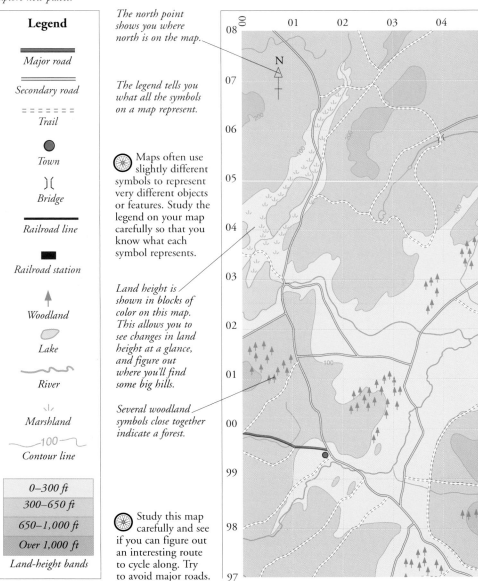

Understanding contours

One of the most noticeable differences between a map and the land it describes is that a map is flat, but the land is bumpy. Contours solve this problem. A contour line is an imaginary line that follows the ground surface at a specific level. When the contour line is drawn on the map, the land height appears next to it. A series of contour lines helps you figure out where the ground changes height.

How contour lines are measured and drawn on a map

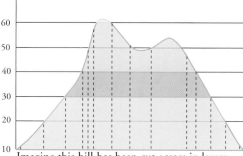

Imagine this hill has been cut across in layers every 33 ft (10 m). Draw an imaginary line around the edge of each layer.

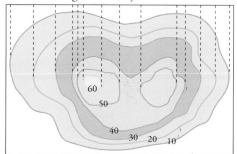

When these imaginary lines are placed together on a map, they form contour lines. Follow the contour lines to figure out the shape of the hill.

Most maps have a grid of squares on them. The lines are drawn at regular intervals and are numbered so that you can refer to any point on the map by giving these numbers.

If contour lines are close together on the map, the changes in land height are very steep. If they are widely spaced, the change is much more gradual.

When you give a grid reference, write down the vertical gridline number that is closest to the point first, and then the horizontal line number.

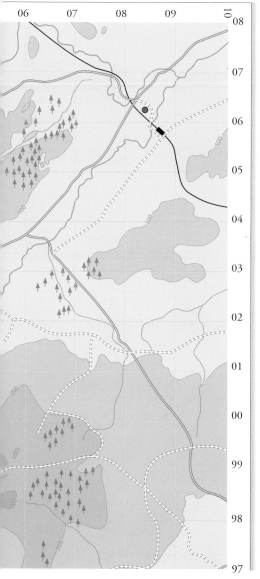

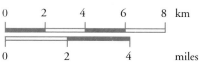

Scale bar

Everything on a map is scaled down and drawn to a fraction of its real size. On this map the scale is 1:50,000. This means that 1 ¼ inch on the map is equal to 1 mile on the ground.

Planning your route

Before setting off on any cycling trip, you need to plan your route. This is especially important if you are exploring a new area. When choosing your route, think about how long you want to be out on the road or trail. Remember that rough terrain will take longer to cycle over than flat terrain.

Always take the time to plan your route before setting off on your trip.

Materials

String

Waterproof tape

Poster board

Plastic sleeves

Scissors

Hints and tips

Leave a copy of your route, and indicate the time you expect to arrive back, with an adult. If you are late coming back, he or she will know where to look for you.

Make a plastic sleeve by folding a sheet of plastic in half. Tape one long and one short side.

How to make a map case

This map case will protect your map. You can also mark your route on the case, so you will not have to mark up your map.

1 Seal the sides of two plastic sleeves as shown on the right. Then join the sleeves together on one side by taping the open end of one sleeve to the short, closed end of the other sleeve.

2 Strengthen the corners of the plastic sleeves as shown on the right. With a pair of scissors carefully make one hole in each corner of the joined sleeves.

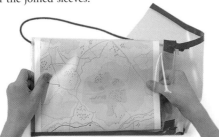

3 Make a carrying strap as shown on the right. The bottom sleeve will form the map case. Fold your map so that it fits into the case and you can see the area you plan to cycle through.

More details on how to make a map case with plastic sleeves

Wrap a strip of waterproof tape along the long open side of the plastic sleeve to seal it.

Fold the sleeves over so the top sleeve is open at the bottom. Tape the top corners for extra strength.

Thread a piece of string through the holes to make a loop and hang the case around your neck.

The poster board will become your route card. Slide it into the top sleeve and seal with tape.

Which way?

Once you know how long you want your trip to last, choose a destination, for example a hilltop with a good view. Then figure out the best way to get there and back. Try to avoid major roads and look for interesting trails to follow instead.

Use a water-soluble pen or crayon to draw your planned route on the plastic map case.

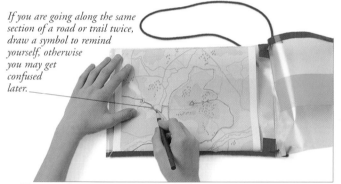

1 Decide where you will start your route if you're not starting straight from home. Choose a point that is close to a trail or secondary road so that you will not have to cycle along major roads for long.

If you are going along the same section of a road or trail twice, draw a symbol to remind yourself, otherwise you may get confused later.

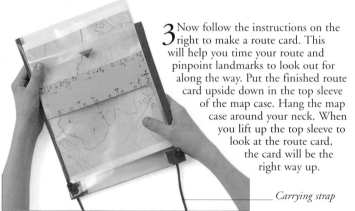

2 Try to make your route circular so that you won't double back on yourself. On this route, we have gone down the hill and then followed a trail that goes around the other side of the hill to return to the starting point.

3 Now follow the instructions on the right to make a route card. This will help you time your route and pinpoint landmarks to look out for along the way. Put the finished route card upside down in the top sleeve of the map case. Hang the map case around your neck. When you lift up the top sleeve to look at the route card, the card will be the right way up.

Carrying strap

How to make a route card to help you follow your route

Take the card out of the sleeve. Put one corner on your starting point. Draw a symbol to represent it.

Pivot the card so it aligns with the route. Mark on the card the point at which the route bends.

Continue pivoting and aligning the card with your route. Draw a symbol for each point.

Follow the route all the way around the card. Draw arrows to remind you of the direction.

Align the finished route card with the map's scale bar. Divide the route up into one-mile sections.

See page 30 to find out how and why you may need to shorten your route.

Navigating on your bike

You never know what might to happen on a trip, so always be prepared. Make sure you can shorten your route in case you get tired or the weather changes. Also, learn how to use a map and compass together so that you can check you are going in the right direction. This skill is called navigation.

Check your map and route card often to ensure you do not get lost.

Planning escape routes

Study your route carefully and try to figure out where you may get tired. If you plan to cycle up several hills, it is a good idea to make sure you have a number of escape routes near the hills. An escape route is another route you could follow to shorten your trip. If you think weather conditions may change, choose several escape routes so you can shorten your trip at any time. Study the escape routes shown on the map below.

⊙ You also need to think carefully about your rest stops. Try to choose places that either give you a good view, provide shelter, or are interesting.

Examples of interesting places to stop for a rest

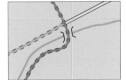

A bridge is often a good place to rest. It is an obvious landmark to use when checking your map.

If there is a pond along your route, try to take a rest next to it so that you can study the wildlife.

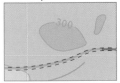

Cycling to the top of a hill is very challenging. When you rest at the top, you'll have an excellent view.

A wooded area will provide shade, which is very welcome on a hot summers day.

The red lines represent the planned routes.

The green lines represent the escape routes.

If your escape route takes you along a major road, be extra careful.

This escape route may not look very short, but it is on flat ground, so will be easy to cycle along.

Choose an escape route near your lunch stop. If you find you are tired after lunch, you can then go home.

More details on how to use a map and compass to navigate

The edge of the compass should align with your starting point and the first section of the route.

Make sure that the arrow on the ruler section of the compass is pointing in the direction you want to go.

The needle that moves around when you move your compass always points north.

Having checked your direction, follow the route marked on the map.

Finding your way

If you are cycling in a new area, use your map and compass often to check you are going in the right direction.

1 Place your compass on your map over your starting point (see the detailed instructions on the left). Keep the map flat.

Practice using a compass before you set off on a trip.

2 Turn the dial on your compass around until the red arrow on the dial runs parallel with the upright, or vertical, grid lines on the map.

3 Keep the compass firmly on the map and turn the map around until the needle that moves (see the detailed instructions on the left) sits on top of the arrow on the compass dial. You are now facing north. Look at the arrow on the ruler section of the compass. It is pointing in the direction you need to go.

Hints and tips

A compass has a magnet in it, so make sure you do not put it near anything made of metal. If you do, it will not work properly.

When the map is pointing north, the writing and symbols will be the right way up.

If you are cycling on a windy day, try to cycle into the wind on the way out. By doing this, you will have the wind behind you on the way home.

What is a bike computer?

A bike computer is a very useful accessory. It fits on your handlebars where you can always see its small screen.

You can use a computer to tell you how fast you are traveling, how far you have gone, and your average speed.

Bike computers are usually waterproof, so you can keep them on your bike all the time.

Most computers will add up how many miles or kilometers you have cycled.

The computer attaches to the handlebars of your bike. A cable runs from the computer down to a sensor on the front wheel. It measures how many times a minute the wheel is turning.

Many computers tell you the time, so you do not need to wear a watch.

Push the buttons on the computer to use the different functions.

Practice cycling with a loaded bike before you set off on an expedition.

Preparing for your trip

Having chosen your route, you need to pack your gear. Only pack what you really need – an overloaded bike is difficult to ride. But be sure to be prepared for changes in the weather. The bike cover shown below will keep you dry if it rains and can also double-up as a picnic blanket in sunny weather.

Materials for the bike cover

String **Tape**

Stapler

Pebbles

Scissors

Plastic sheet

Hints and tips

Remember to take your map, route card, and compass with you on your trip.

Pannier racks are assembled with either a regular or Allen wrench.

Make sure that both pannier bags weigh the same amount. If they do not, you will find it difficult to balance.

Put heavy items at the bottom of the panniers.

Making a bike cover

This bike cover is very quick to make and light to carry, so take it with you on all your trips.

1 Lean your bike against a solid object, such as a tree trunk. Tie your bike to the trunk by wrapping a piece of string or a bungee cord around the trunk and the seat post of your bike.

Short side of sheet

2 Get the plastic sheet and cut it into an oblong 10 ft x 6 ½ ft (3 m x 2 m). Pull one of the short sides up over the front of your bike.

Cut the sheet by the trunk.

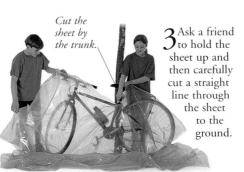

3 Ask a friend to hold the sheet up and then carefully cut a straight line through the sheet to the ground.

More details on how to make a bike cover with a sheet of plastic

To make the bike cover completely watertight, secure all the folds with a piece of tape.

Staple the taped folds for extra strength and then put a second piece of tape over the tops of the staples.

Pull out each corner of the bike cover and wrap a pebble in the plastic.

Hold the pebble in place by tying a piece of string around it. Keep one end of each string long.

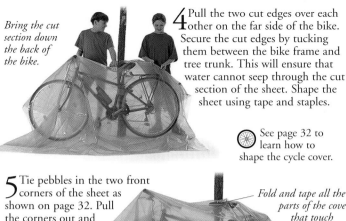

Bring the cut section down the back of the bike.

4 Pull the two cut edges over each other on the far side of the bike. Secure the cut edges by tucking them between the bike frame and tree trunk. This will ensure that water cannot seep through the cut section of the sheet. Shape the sheet using tape and staples.

See page 32 to learn how to shape the cycle cover.

How to attach a pannier rack to your rear wheel

Screw all the parts of the rack together following the manufacturer's instructions.

5 Tie pebbles in the two front corners of the sheet as shown on page 32. Pull the corners out and tie the long ends of the strings to secure objects.

Fold and tape all the parts of the cover that touch your bike.

Leave a gap between the sheet and ground to let air in.

Tie the string to another tree trunk.

Screw the bottom of the pannier rack to the hole on the rear dropout. Do not tighten the screw yet.

Packing for your trip

Whether your trip is going to last one hour or a whole day, you will need to take provisions with you. If you are going on a short trip, take something to drink, a waterproof jacket, a tool kit, and a first aid kit with you. For longer trips, include the items shown here in your pannier bags.

Take a pair of warm pants, such as sweatpants, in case it gets cold.

A bandanna will help keep you cool in the summer and warm in the winter.

Pack a spare pair of socks. If your feet get cold, you can put the socks over your shoes.

Record your trips in a logbook.

Always take a first aid kit with you – be sure you know how to use it.

These pannier bags clip onto the sides of a pannier rack.

Lever the pannier rack over the wheel so that the flat top of the rack sits over the top of the wheel.

Choose high-energy foods that are easy to carry for your lunch. Sandwiches, chips, and fruit are ideal.

Pack sunglasses if it is likely to be a sunny day.

Take toe-clip straps to secure loose items on your bike.

If you plan to cycle at dawn or dusk, pack reflective bands. Wear them whenever the light is dim.

Be prepared for changes in the weather by packing a waterproof jacket.

Attach the front "arms" of the rack to the seat stay. Tighten the screws at the seat stay and rear dropout.

The panniers will hang down the sides of the rack, so you can attach extra items to the top.

Some pannier bags are joined together. The join sits over the top of the pannier rack.

Recording your trip

Since you've put in a lot effort planning your route and preparing for your trip, why not keep a record of it in a logbook? Your logbook can contain lots of information, such as where you go, when, and who comes along on a trip. It can also have a diary section for noting special things you do and see along the way.

Always try to make room for your logbook in your panniers.

Materials for the logbook & pocket

Scissors | Crayons

String

Sheets of paper

Small piece of plastic

Plastic sheet

Pen

Needle | Thread

Material

Hints and tips

Sew a back pocket on your T-shirt to store items you use a lot. This way you won't have to get off your bike and hunt through your panniers.

Hemming the material on your pocket will stop the edges from fraying.

Making a logbook
Make this logbook at home following the instructions below.

1 Cut the plastic sheet to size, fold the sheets of paper in half, and pierce holes in the paper and plastic as shown on the right.

2 Put the folded paper on the plastic, making sure all the holes line up. Thread a piece of string through the holes as shown on the right.

Tie a bow in the string on the outside of your logbook.

The plastic sheet makes your logbook waterproof.

3 The basic logbook is now completed. Follow the instructions on page 35 to add a pocket to store your pens in.

More details on how to make a logbook

Cut the plastic sheet so that it is about 1 in (2 cm) wider all around than the sheets of paper.

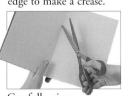

Fold the pieces of paper in half and press down firmly along the folded edge to make a crease.

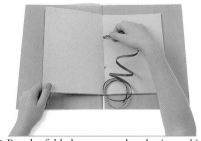

Carefully pierce two holes in the folded section of the paper. Ask an adult to help you.

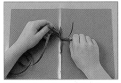

Thread a piece of string through the holes in the folded paper and then through the plastic.

How to make a pocket to store pens in the logbook

Tape the small piece of plastic to the top sheet of paper. Remember to leave the top open!

Make sure that the pocket is deep and wide enough for your pens and crayons.

Fold over the long edges of the plastic cover and tape them down to keep the logbook closed.

Remember to take plenty to drink on your trip.

Filling in your logbook

It is entirely up to you what you put in your logbook. Here are some examples of things you could record.

1 Stick a photograph of you and your friends in your logbook. Make a note underneath it of your planned route and the date. This will mark the starting point of your trip.

2 Keep a record of what you see along your route. You could press leaves in your logbook, record the wildlife, and stick down postcards of places you visit.

3 When you stop for a rest on your trip, make notes in your logbook. You can record where you stopped for lunch, what the weather was like, if you found the route tiring – anything you think is interesting.

When you take a break, look at your map to check where you are going next.

How to make a pocket on a T-shirt to store extra items

Cut an oblong of material that is almost the width of your T-shirt. Hem the edges of the material.

Sew the hemmed material to the back of your T-shirt. Leave the top edge open.

Make two pockets by sewing a line up the middle of the material and the T-shirt.

Store soft items in your pocket, such as your gloves, bandanna, and any snacks.

 Sit on the bike cover you made on page 32.

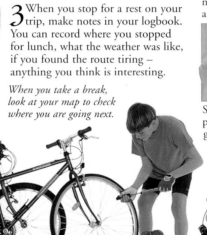

Bike cleaning and oiling

It is amazing how much dirt can cling to your bike when you are cycling off-road. Cleaning and oiling your bike regularly will stop the dirt from building up and will also make it run better. You should give your bike a wash after every muddy ride, and give it a thorough cleaning several times a year.

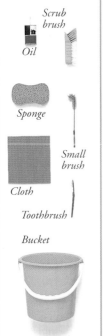

You must clean and oil your bike after every muddy ride.

Materials

Scrub brush

Oil

Sponge

Small brush

Cloth

Toothbrush

Bucket

Cleaning your bike

Turn your bike upside down so that you do not have to lean it against anything. Fill a bucket with warm, soapy water and wash the whole bike, paying particular attention to the areas shown below.

You could rest the seat on a cloth so that you do not scratch it.

Use a toothbrush to clean the wheel spokes and hubs. If dirt enters the hubs, the bearings will not run smoothly.

Clean the chainrings with a stiff brush. Your gear changes may become jerky if you leave dirt here.

Remember to clean the brake pads.

Store all your cleaning materials together.

Use a soft sponge and plenty of soapy water to clean the frame. This way you won't scratch the paintwork.

Remember to rinse the soapy water off your bike.

Use a small brush to clean the sprockets. Be careful when doing this because the sprockets are very sharp.

Hints and tips

You can use a hose to wash off most of the mud if you are careful not to spray any of the moving parts.

Avoid using a vegetable-based oil on your bike because it will leave a sticky residue.

Oiling your bike

After you have given your bike a thorough cleaning, you will need to replace the oil you have washed off. This will keep all the moving parts of your bike working smoothly and prevent rusting. Turn your bike right-side up for oiling, otherwise the oil will drip down onto your handlebars and seat.

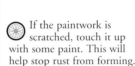

Oil the chain in sections. Push the pedal backward to move the chain around so you can oil a new section.

✳ If the paintwork is scratched, touch it up with some paint. This will help stop rust from forming.

Oil the moving parts of the brakes. If you spill any oil on the brake pads, clean it off thoroughly with soapy water.

If you get oil on the brake pads, they will not work properly.

Check that the quick-release levers and other fittings on your bike are properly secured.

Push the arm of the rear derailleur down so that you can oil the jockey wheels – the two pulley wheels in the arm.

✳ Keep an eye out for any parts on your bike that need adjusting or repairing.

Oil the moving parts of the front and rear derailleurs. Check which parts move by moving the gear shifters.

✳ Always make sure your bike is completely dry before you start oiling it. Otherwise the oil may not reach the bearings and the other moving parts.

QR levers

Quick-release levers are often called QR levers for short. These fittings are very popular on bike wheels and seats because they eliminate the need for tools. However, if you do not close a lever correctly, it could be dangerous.

The correct position
When the lever is closed correctly, it will curve inward toward the wheel.

The incorrect position
If the lever curves outward, it is open and not locked, making your bike unsafe to ride.

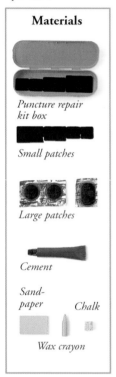

Repairing a puncture

Each wheel has an inner tube full of air. If you get a puncture, you will have to replace or repair this tube. Repairing an inner tube can take some time, so take a spare one with you. Then, if you do get a puncture, you can replace the inner tube with your spare tube, and repair the damaged one at home.

Cycling over rough ground risks getting a puncture.

Materials

Puncture repair kit box

Small patches

Large patches

Cement

Sand-paper   *Chalk*

Wax crayon

Hints and tips

You will also need your basic tool kit to repair a puncture. Page 12 shows you what you need in your tool kit.

Removing a rear wheel is complicated, so ask an adult to help you with a rear tire puncture.

Changing tubes

The instructions below show you how to replace an inner tube.

1 Ask a friend to hold the bike. Release the wheel from the front fork. You may just need to open a quick-release lever, otherwise use a wrench.

Lean the tire against you to keep it still.

2 Slide one tire lever between the tire and wheel rim. Repeat with a second tire lever a little farther around the wheel. Push down on the tire levers to pry one side of the tire off the wheel rim.

Leave one side of the tire on the wheel.

3 Release any air left in the inner tube through the valve, see right, and pull the inner tube out.

More details on how to replace an inner tube

Unclip the brake cable from the brake arm so that you can slide the wheel out more easily.

If your wheels are not attached to your bike by quick-release levers, you will need to use a wrench.

To release the air on a schraeder valve, push down on the valve pin.

Release the air on a presta valve by unscrewing the top and pushing in the valve pin.

More details on how to replace an inner tube (continued)

Feel along the inside of the tire to find out what caused the puncture, then remove it.

Push the tire over the top of the wheel rim so that it slots back into place and holds the inner tube in.

Check that the inner tube is covered by the tire and is not pinched between the tire and wheel rim.

To find the hole in a damaged inner tube, pump a little air into it and immerse the tube in some water. Air bubbles will come out of the hole.

Pump a little air into the spare tube to help prevent it from catching between the tire and wheel rim.

4 Push the inner tube valve into its hole in the wheel rim. Slide the new inner tube between the tire and wheel rim. Push the tire back in place, as shown on the left.

Ask a friend to hold the wheel steady.

Make sure your bike pump has the correct needle for the valves on your bike.

5 Pump up the tube and check that it is not bulging off the rim anywhere. If it is, stop pumping and straighten the inner tube before continuing.

Remember to take the punctured inner tube home with you.

6 You are now ready to put the wheel back on the bike. Slide the wheel between the front fork and brake pads and secure the wheel to the front fork. Clip the brake cables back onto the brake arms. Check that your brakes are working properly.

Hold the tire between your legs to keep it upright.

See page 37 to learn how to check that your quick-release levers are in the correct position.

How to repair a damaged inner tube with a puncture repair kit

Use the wax crayon to draw a circle around the hole in the inner tube so you can see it easily.

Sand the smooth surface of the inner tube around the hole with the sandpaper to make it rough.

Spread a small amount of cement around the hole. Leave it to dry for five minutes.

Remove the foil backing from a patch and stick it over the hole. Leave it to dry for five more minutes.

Peel off the cellophane covering. Sprinkle chalk dust over the patch to soak up any extra glue.

The dust will help you slide the inner tube back into the tire. Rub the chalk over the sandpaper to make dust.

Maintaining your bike

Cycling off-road causes a lot of wear and tear on your bike. If you do not take care of all the parts they will wear out quickly. By performing the basic maintenance checks shown on these pages, the parts of your bike will last longer and you may avoid expensive repairs.

Keep your tools together in a tool pouch so you can find them easily.

Checking the cranks

The cranks hold your pedals in place. They are low to the ground and can become loose when cycling over rough ground. Check the cranks regularly – if you cycle with a loose crank, it could become damaged. To test your cranks, grip each crank and try to rock them from side to side.

Hints and tips

⊛ Clean your tools with an old rag each time you use them.

⊛ If you are not sure which tool to use for a specific job, ask at your local bike shop.

⊛ Whenever you take anything apart, lay out the separate pieces in the order they came off the bike.

⊛ When you tighten a crank, remember to hold the pedal securely with one hand.

⊛ The chainring bolts keep your chainring in place.

⊛ Never use a screwdriver instead of an Allen wrench or you will damage the bolt.

Tightening the cranks

If there is a dust cap covering the crank attachment, remove it and put it in a safe place. Check to see how your cranks are attached and follow the instructions below to secure them.

1 Cranks attached with a sunken nut need a special wrench that fits into the recess. Turn the wrench clockwise to tighten the nut.

2 To tighten a crank attached with an Allen wrench, use the correct-sized Allen wrench and turn it clockwise.

⊛ Use an Allen wrench to check that the chainring bolts are not loose.

⊛ You may need adult help to get the cranks tight enough.

How to recognize a worn brake cable and brake pad

Check the brake cables regularly for signs of fraying. If you find any, the cable needs replacing.

This brake pad has worn down so much that it will not work effectively.

Adjusting your handlebars

Before you set off on a ride, you need to know how to adjust the height and angle of your handlebars so that you can adapt your bike to your size. It is also important to check that the stem is securely tightened. Put the front wheel between your knees and try to twist the handlebars. If the stem moves, the bolt needs tightening.

⊛ The stem clamp is at the front of the handlebars.

Stem bolt

Stem

How to adjust the height and angle of the handlebars

Loosen the stem bolt and raise or lower the stem to the correct height before tightening the bolt again.

Loosen the stem clamp to rotate the handlebars. Remember to tighten the stem clamp afterward.

⊛ The stem should have a safety line marked on it. You can move the handlebars safely up to this maximum point.

Grip the front wheel between your legs to steady the bike.

⊛ The stem bolt and clamp are loosened with either a regular or Allen wrench.

⊛ The rear derailleur and chainring are fairly far apart, so ask a friend to help you.

How to release the tension in the chain

Push the arm of the rear derailleur forward to push the chain forward and make it hang loosely.

When you turn the pedal backward, keep the chain pulled away from the chainring.

Unjamming a chain

If your chain gets jammed, you must release it immediately, otherwise the chain could break. It should be easy to release a jammed chain, but you will need adult help to repair a broken one.

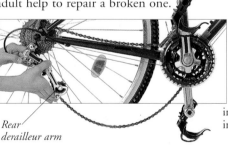

Rear derailleur arm

2 Hold the chain and turn the pedal backward slowly until the chain has moved all the way around the chainring and rear derailleur. This will release the jammed chain. Release the arm of the rear derailleur so it pulls the chain tight.

⊛ Turn the pedals backward when releasing the chain – this will not push the back wheel around. If you push the pedals forward, the wheel will turn, too.

1 Before you can find the cause of the jammed chain, you will need to release the tension in the chain (see the instructions on the left).

First aid

No matter how carefully you cycle, accidents can still happen. The very nature of cycling means that you will usually be away from home when an accident occurs, so always take a first aid kit with you. The techniques shown on these pages show you how to deal with the most common cycling injuries.

Make your first aid kit waterproof by packing it in a plastic bag.

Materials

Triangular bandage to tie arm slings

Scissors to cut bandages

Bandages of varying sizes

Safety pins for securing slings

Gauze pad for treating cuts and scrapes.

Antiseptic cream to clean cuts and scrapes.

An object in your eye

If you get a piece of grit in your eye when you are cycling, you will soon feel it. Your eye will water and feel sore. Ask a friend to help you remove the foreign body.

Tilt the head back.

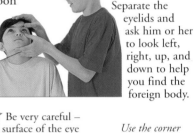

1 Sit the patient down, facing toward the light. Separate the eyelids and ask him or her to look left, right, up, and down to help you find the foreign body.

⭐ Be very careful – the surface of the eye is very delicate.

Aim for the inner corner of the eye.

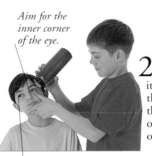

2 If you can see the foreign body, wash it out with water. Tilt the head back and then pour plenty of clean water over the eye.

Use the corner of a clean gauze pad or bandage to remove the foreign body.

Ask the patient to look away from the water.

3 If the foreign body does not wash out, you can use the corner of a clean cloth to lift it out.

4 Sometimes you will not be able to see the foreign body, for example when it is under the eyelid. In these cases, ask the patient to lift her upper eyelid slightly outward and then downward over the lower eyelid. This should clear away the foreign body.

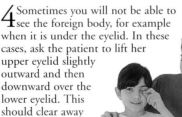

Hints and tips

If you cannot remove the foreign body from your patient's eye easily, get adult help immediately.

Put round-ended scissors in your first aid kit. If you use scissors with sharp ends, they could make a hole in the plastic bag.

How to tie an arm sling with a triangular bandage

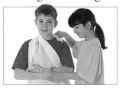

Place the bandage between the patient's bent injured arm and chest. Bring one end up around the neck.

Bring the lower end of the bandage up over the front of the forearm to meet the end at the shoulder.

Tie the two ends together just below the shoulder. Pin any loose fabric to the bandage with a safety pin.

⚙ Use an arm sling to support an injured elbow, lower arm, or wrist.

⭐ Be careful not to prick the patient with the safety pin.

How to tie an elevation sling

If the patient has hurt his or her collar-bone or shoulder, you will need to support the arm on the injured side with an elevation sling.

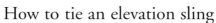

1 Bring the arm on the injured side up and across the patient's body. Ask him or her to support the elbow with the opposite hand.

Hold the top corner at the shoulder.

Support the arm on the injured side.

2 Lay the triangular bandage over the injured arm. Make sure the top of the long edge is hanging on the uninjured side so that when you secure the bandage, the knot sits on this side.

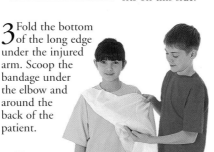

3 Fold the bottom of the long edge under the injured arm. Scoop the bandage under the elbow and around the back of the patient.

4 Bring the long edge of the bandage diagonally across the patient's back and up to the far shoulder. Make sure the elbow is held securely in the fabric.

5 Tie the two ends of the bandage just in front of the shoulder on the uninjured side. Gather any loose fabric and secure it with a safety pin.

⚙ If you do not have a safety pin, twist the loose fabric and tuck it inside the sling at the elbow.

How to treat cuts and scrapes with a clean gauze pad

Gently wash the injured area with clean water. Use a clean gauze pad or soft cloth.

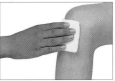

Try to wash off any bits of dirt or gravel. Be very gentle – this may cause some fresh bleeding.

Get a clean gauze pad and apply pressure to the injured area to stop any bleeding.

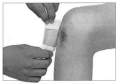

Put an adhesive bandage over the injured area. Be sure it has a pad large enough to cover the wound.

Rules for the road

To make sure that all your cycle trips are enjoyable and safe, it is important to follow a few golden rules. When cycling in a group, always follow the instructions given by the leader. Respect the countryside you are traveling through, and be considerate of other people and animals along your route.

Be considerate so others can enjoy safe rides after you.

When you reach the top of a hill, take time to enjoy the view with your friends before cycling down again.

If the road or trail is wide and smooth, you can cycle two abreast. However, if it is narrow or rough, or you are cycling around obstacles or up and down hills, cycle in single file. When you cycle up a hill, keep your distance from the other cyclists and wait at the top for the rest of your group before cycling down the hill.

Most serious accidents happen when cyclists go too fast downhill. Keep your distance from the cyclist in front and feather your brakes to keep your speed under control. This will reduce the risk of skidding.

In good cycling conditions, keep a bike-lengths gap from the rider in front.

The leader should insist on regular rest stops.

Even if you are cycling along a straight and smooth path, there are still certain guidelines you need to follow. One experienced cyclist should lead the group and a second experienced cyclist should stay at the back of the group to make sure no one is getting too tired or being left behind. Try to cycle with people who have a similar amount of cycling experience.

If the group is not cycling fast enough for you, ask the leader if you can cycle ahead for a few minutes and then double back to the group. This will allow you to cycle faster and farther while still staying close to the group.

Outdoor Code for cyclists

Always follow the Outdoor Code when you are out on roads and trails. This will keep the countryside a place that everyone can enjoy. The points mentioned on these pages are especially important for cyclists, so make sure you learn them before you set off.

Some roads and trails are not open to cyclists. Always check that you are allowed to cycle along a road or trail before you do so.

Take your empty drink cans and other garbage home with you. Do not litter the countryside – you could harm wildlife.

Do not light fires – they can easily get out of control.

Leave gates the way you found them – either open or closed. If a gate has been left open, there is almost certainly a reason for it.

Stay on marked roads and trails and never ride through fields because you may damage crops.

Be considerate toward all animals you meet. If you scare them, they could hurt you or themselves.

Be sure to let any walkers you meet on a path pass you. Get off your bike if the path is narrow.

Do not pick flowers or uproot plants. It is very destructive, and in some places it is even illegal. Take photographs or make drawings to record what you have seen instead.

Wear brightly colored clothes so that you can be seen easily. This is very important on cloudy days and in dim light.

Avoid roads and trails that run along an unfenced water's edge. If you end up on one and the path is narrow, get off your bike and push it until you reach a safer trail.

Glossary

Allen wrench
A six-sided L-shaped tool used to adjust an Allen bolt. Bike gears and brakes are often secured with Allen bolts.

Bearing
Found in the wheel hub, pedals, headset, and bottom bracket. Bearings contain small steel balls that enable the moving parts to work smoothly.

Bike computer
A small device attached to your handlebars and front wheel. It can measure how quickly you are cycling, your average speed, how far you have traveled, and

usually tells you the time. Some bike computers can even tell your pedal cadence.

Bottom bracket
The bracket that joins the seat tube to the down tube and houses the cranks.

Brake pads
The two rubber blocks that touch the wheel rim to slow down the bike when the brake levers are pulled.

Chicane
A very narrow path that requires good balancing skills

to cycle through. *It is pronounced shecane.*

Crank
The arm that joins one pedal to the bottom bracket and gear system.

Derailleurs
Transmission mechanisms that guide the chain between the chainrings at the front by the seat tube and the sprockets at the rear wheel.

Dust cap
A protective covering found on an inner tube valve and on the crank attachment.

Feathering
A way of braking by pulling the brakes on and off several times in quick succession. This kind of braking reduces the risk of skidding when cycling downhill.

Freewheel
To cycle without pedaling. This technique is used for coasting down hills.

Front derailleur
The part of the transmission system that is attached to the seat tube. It moves the chain from one chainring to another.

Headset
Two-part bearing assembly that holds the steering tube in the head tube.

Head tube
Tube in which the steering tube rotates by means of the headset bearings.

Hub
The center of a wheel. It contains bearings and an axle around which the wheel turns.

Jockey wheels
The two pulley wheels found in the arm of the rear derailleur. They are used to guide the chain.

Logbook
A diary for recording the details of your trip.

Navigation
How to find your way, usually with a map and compass.

Pannier bag
A bag that can be attached to the front or rear of a bike. A pair of pannier bags hangs from a rack down either side of the front or back wheel.

Pedal cadence
The speed at which the pedals are pushed around. The ideal pedal cadence is about 90 turns a minute.

Quick-release lever
Also known as a QR lever, it is an-easy-to-adjust way of holding the wheels and seat in place. QR levers are found on most modern bikes.

Rear derailleur
The part of the transmission system attached to the right-hand rear dropout. It moves the chain from one sprocket to another.

Slalom
A race that requires cycling around a series of objects. *It is pronounced slawlom.*

Spoke
A thin rod that runs from a wheel hub to the rim.

Stem
Attaches the handlebars to the frame via the steering tube.

Tire lever
A plastic or metal lever that is used to pry a tire from the wheel rim.

Toe clip
A device attached to a pedal. It is designed to keep your foot in the right place on the pedal.

Toe-in
The angle at which a brake pad touches the wheel rim.

Valve
The device on an inner tube through which you can pump or release air.

Useful addresses

American Bicycle Association
PO Box 718
Chandler, AZ 85244

Bicycle Federation of America
1506 21st Street, NW
Ste. 200
Washington D.C. 20036

International Randonneurs
Old Engine House No. 2
727 N. Salina Street
Syracuse, NY 13208

League of American Bicyclists
190 West Ostend Street, 120
Baltimore, MD 21230

National Bicycle League
3958 Brown Park Drive, Ste. D.
Hilliard, OH 43026

USA Cycling, Inc.
1 Olympia Plaza
Colorado Springs, CO 80909

Brooks Country Cycling Tours
140 West 83rd Street
New York, NY 10024

Century Road Club
215 West 98th Street
New York, NY 10025

New York Cycling Club
80 8th Avenue
New York, NY 10011

Dahon California, Inc.
833 Meridian Street
Duarde, CA 91010

International Mountain Bicycling
Association
Rte. 2, Box 303
Bishop, CA 93514

Worldwide Cycle Supply
11 Constance Court
Hauppague, NY 11788

Index

A, B

accessories 13
Allen wrench 12, 46
arm sling, how
  to tie 43
bandanna 10, 11
baton, how to
  make 25
bearings 9, 46
bell 13
bike computer
  31, 46
bottom bracket 46
brake pads 15, 46
braking 15, 19
bungee cords 12,
  13

C

carrying your
bike 20
chain 8, 41
chain tool 12
chicane 18, 19,
  46
compass, how
  to use 31
cones, how to
  make 16
contours 27
crank 9, 40, 46

cycle cover,
  how to make
  32, 33
cycle limbo 21
cycle polo 25
cycle relay 24

D, E

derailleur gear
  system 8, 46
downhill cycling 19
elevation sling,
  how to tie 43
dust cap 46
emergency stops 19
escape routes 30

F, G

feathering 15, 46
first aid kit 33, 42
foot position 15
freewheel 19, 46
front derailleur 8,
  46
gear lever 9, 17
gears, how to
  change 17
glasses 11
gloves 11
grid line 27

H, I, J, K

handlebars, how
  to adjust 41
headset 9, 46
helmet 10
high gear 17
hills 19, 44
hopping over
  logs 21

hub 46
inner tube 12, 38
jockey wheels 37,
  41, 46

L, M, N

legend 26
lock 13
logbook 34,
  35, 46
low gear 17
map case, how
  to make 28
middle gear 17
mountain bike
  9
navigation 30,
  46

O, P

oiling your
  bike 37
pannier bag
  13, 33, 46
pannier rack
  13, 33
pedal cadence
  16, 46
pump 12
puncture, how
  to repair 38, 39
puncture repair
  kit 13
pre-ride checks
  14, 40, 41

presta valve 38

Q, R, S

quick-release
  lever 37, 47
racing bike 9
rear derailleur 8, 47
reflector 8, 9, 13
route card, how
  to make 29
seat, how to
  adjust 14
shraeder valve 38
slalom 16, 47
slow race 25
spoke 47
spoke key 12
stem 47

T, U, V

tire lever 12, 38, 47
toe clip 9, 15, 47

toe-clip strap 13
toe-in 47
tool kit 12
tool pouch, how
  to make 13
uphill cycling 19
valve 38, 47

W, X, Y, Z

water bottle 11, 13
wrench 12

Acknowledgments

DK would like to thank:

Trek UK for lending the bikes, Dr. Rachel Carroll
and Dr. Simon Carroll for advice on first
aid procedures, and Stan Turner, Senior Coach,
at Lee Valley Cycle Circuit.
Cartography: David Roberts, Jane Voss
Illustrations: Nick Hewetson
Picture research: Sharon Southren
Picture credits: T top; B bottom; C center;
L left; R right; A above

J. Allan Cash Photo Library: 23 TL, CL, CLB 26T,
45CLA, CA, CB, CRA, CRB, BL; Allsport UK Ltd
Pascal Rondeau: 36T; Anton Want: 22T; Robert
Harding Picture Library/Ian Tomlinson
Photography: 44T; Images Colour Library: 20T,
23CLA; Pendle Engineering, Nelson, Lancashire:
9TL; Raleigh Industries: 9CR; Stockfile/Steven
Behr: 8T, 10T, 16T, 24T, 28T, 30T, 38T, 44C, BR,
BL, 45TR, CLB, BR; Zefa Pictures Allstock: 32T